流行樂隊

The Beatles

流行樂隊 The Beatles

責任編輯：張倩儀

出　　版：商務印書館（香港）有限公司

　　　　　香港筲箕灣耀興道 3 號東滙廣場 8 樓

　　　　　http://www.commercialpress.com.hk

發　　行：香港聯合書刊物流有限公司

　　　　　香港新界大埔汀麗路 36 號中華商務印刷大廈 3 字樓

印　　刷：中華商務彩色印刷有限公司

　　　　　香港新界大埔汀麗路 36 號中華商務印刷大廈

版　　次：2010 年 3 月第 1 版第 1 次印刷

　　　　　© 2010 商務印書館（香港）有限公司

　　　　　ISBN 978 962 07 1892 2

　　　　　Printed in Hong Kong

本書由 Saddleback Educational Publishing 授權出
版，僅限亞洲及北美地區銷售。

流行樂隊

The Beatles

商務印書館

Contents

Graphic biography of the Beatles   *1*

Usage guide for exercise   *26*

Exercise   *27*

Answers   *53*

Vocabulary

    General vocabulary   *54*

    Music and performance related vocabulary *55*

Activities

    The Beatles Hits   *56*

"The thing is, we're all really the same person. We're just four parts of the one." Paul McCartney

JOHN LENNON

PAUL McCARTNEY

GEORGE HARRISON

RINGO STARR

The Beatles charted 20 number one singles in the United States—three more than Elvis.

Liverpool is the industrial city in England where the Beatles grew up. In those days there were more people out of work there than in any other place in the country.

Merseyside was a section of Liverpool. It had many clubs where small bands played for teenagers. As many as 350 bands played there for very little money.

The *Mersey Beat* was a newspaper known only to local beat music lovers until the Beatles made Liverpool, and the newspaper, famous.

Liverpool had one of the first rock concerts. Alan Williams, the Beatles first manager, held a fourteen hour pop concert outdoors.

Williams also owned the Jacaranda and the Cavern Club where the Beatles played.

John Lennon

Stay until the baby is born.

John Lennon was born in October 1940. His father came and went from his life frequently.

John went to live with his aunt and uncle when he was about 5 years old.

See, Aunt Mimi, I've written a story for you. And I drew a picture too.

John liked to draw. He also enjoyed listening to music.

When John was eleven, he heard Bill Haley and the Comets on records. Then he discovered the records of Elvis Presley.

Are you listening to "Rock Around the Clock" again?

No, something I just got. A singer named Elvis Presley. He's American and great!

I'm glad you came to see me. I want to ask a favor,▲ Mum. Could you buy me a guitar?

Well, Luv, if I can find an inexpensive one, it's yours.

A guitar's all right, John, but you'll never earn a living from it.

When he was sixteen, John formed a musical group called the Quarrymen. In 1958 his mother was killed by a car. An unhappy John was comforted by his friend Paul McCartney.

▲ British English: favour

4

George Harrison

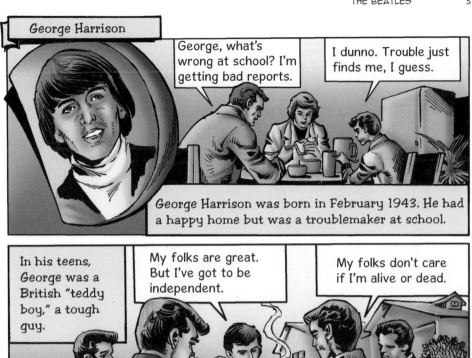

George, what's wrong at school? I'm getting bad reports.

I dunno. Trouble just finds me, I guess.

George Harrison was born in February 1943. He had a happy home but was a troublemaker at school.

In his teens, George was a British "teddy boy," a tough guy.

My folks are great. But I've got to be independent.

My folks don't care if I'm alive or dead.

It took you a long time to get interested in music.

Yeah, but I am now. I'm going to ask mum for a guitar.

George isn't too young for us. I wasn't much older when I joined last year.

He's mighty good on that guitar. So, okay George.

George had no interest in music until he was fourteen. Then Paul McCartney helped him learn to play the guitar.

George joined the Quarrymen in 1958.

John changed the name of the Quarrymen to the Silver Beatles then to the Beatles. The "beat" in Beatles stood for beat music.

The Beatles played at many of the clubs at Merseyside. John, Paul, and George were joined by Stuart Sutcliffe on guitar and Tommy Moore on the drums.

In 1960 Allan Williams, their manager, got them a date to play at a music club in Hamburg, Germany. Tommy was replaced on the drums by Pete Best.

They're making so much noise. They can't hear us.

They don't understand the words in English anyway. Just pound the chords and scream the lyrics.

Okay, imitate the German soldier! March, march!

Let's all imitate the soldiers by high-stepping.

At their drinking and dancing clubs the Germans wanted loud music with a good beat. The Beatles gave them this.

The Germans loved to see the Beatles fool around and make fun of Hitler.

The Beatles were overtired, often playing for eight hours a day, seven days a week. They lived in run-down apartments behind the club where they performed.

While they were playing for a rival nightclub, it was reported that George Harrison was underage. Without a work permit, George was deported home to England. Except for Stuart, who left the band in Hamburg, the rest of the Beatles soon followed George home.

During this time a record store manager, Brian Epstein, was receiving many requests for a group he had never heard of. He started to make inquiries.

Do you have the single "My Bonnie" by a group called the Beatles?

Epstein wanted to see what all they fuss was about. He went to a lunchtime concert at the Cavern Club down the street from his shop. Epstein thought that the band had great potential.

I saw your performance, and I think you have something special. I want to be your manager.

The Beatles agreed and a contract was signed on January 24, 1962.

I wouldn't touch that band with a barge pole! They didn't pay me my commission.

Brian got in touch with Allan Williams, who was no longer the Beatles' manager. He wanted to make sure that Williams did not have any ties to the band.

Epstein set out to change the Beatles' image. He believed a more clean-cut appearance would help the band become more accepted by the general public.

That's not the look I want for all of you. I'll pick new clothes for you to wear!

Epstein tried to interest several recording companies in the Beatles. They turned him down.

You should realize that the Beatles will be bigger than Presley.

Go back to your store business, Brian.

Finally Epstein persuaded George Martin of EMI to listen to the Beatles.

They have something! Yes, I'll be their recording manager.

John, Paul, and George began to be a little upset with Pete Best.

We're a group. Pete forgets that.

He acts like he's a one-man band.

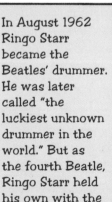

Martin insisted that Pete Best did not fit into the group. Epstein liked Pete but had to let him go.

I'm sorry, Pete. But we have to do what EMI says.

I'll find work.

In August 1962 Ringo Starr became the Beatles' drummer. He was later called "the luckiest unknown drummer in the world." But as the fourth Beatle, Ringo Starr held his own with the others.

Ringo Starr

Ritchie Starkey was born in July 1940. He became Ringo Starr.

I wish I had a brother or sister to play with.

You're enough for us! But I wish we had a bathroom.

Due to several illnesses, Ringo was in and out of the hospital until he was a teenager.

He's still too weak to go home yet.

Ringo met the Beatles in Hamburg. He was playing with another group.

I live behind our club too. Those rooms are worse than these. I'll take the conditions in Liverpool any day.

Do you like Liverpool better because of a hairdresser named Maureen Cox?

Music groups had always recorded material written by someone else.

I can't find a song I like for the Beatles!

Martin let the Beatles record "Love Me Do," written by John and Paul.

A group has never recorded their own song before.

Someday all music groups will record their own songs.

In January 1963 the Beatles recording of "Please Please Me" reached number one on the UK (United Kingdom) charts. In February they went on their first national tour.

I don't believe all this!

Blimey! I wish there were more police!

In May, on their third tour, they had top billing. It was then that Beatlemania—the fans screaming, fainting, and rioting—began.

In October the Beatles appeared on British TV.

They bloody well better let me in. I've been here all day.

The show was called *Sunday Night at the London Palladium.* The theater was mobbed all day.

When they returned from a successful tour of Sweden, the airport was mobbed.

Blimey! I've never seen anything like this in my life!

In November they appeared on The *Royal Variety Show.* Queen Elizabeth, the Queen Mother, Princess Margaret, and Lord Snowden attended.

Those of you in the cheaper seats clap your hands, and those of you in the expensive seats just rattle your jewelry.

There were 250,000 advance orders for the Beatles' second album, *With the Beatles,* beating Elvis Presley's *Blue Hawaii.*

There were one million advance orders for their single "I Want to Hold Your Hand."

In December after the *Beatles Christmas Show,* the *London Times* called the Beatles "the outstanding English composers of 1963."

The *Sunday Times* called them "the greatest composers since Beethoven."

When the Beatles had four solid hits in America, Brian Epstein booked their first United States visit. Ten thousand fans greeted them at Kennedy Airport.

On February 9, 1964, seventy-three million people watched the Beatles on the *Ed Sullivan Show*.

I love their accents!

I just love them!

The Washington Coliseum was jammed for their concert.

They're too noisy to hear us.

When they scream, I just pretend to sing the words.

After the concert, the British Embassy gave a party for them. One girl cut off a piece of Ringo's hair.

After two sell-out shows at Carnegie Hall in New York, the Beatles appeared on a second *Ed Sullivan Show* in Miami Beach.

After it was over, they rested on a private boat.

This is the life!

The police sergeant who was in charge of their security invited them to his house for dinner.

We thought you should see what most of America is like.

The Beatles were mobbed on their return to England.

Their records were all hits. And so was John Lennon's book *In His Own Write*.

How much money is their police protection costing?

It doesn't matter. They are the best export we ever had. I say God bless the Beatles!

I've already read it but want my own copy.

My mum wants a copy. And so does Granny.

HONGKONG

EUROPE

The Beatles toured Europe, Hong Kong, Australia, and New Zealand. They were met by record crowds and screaming fans wherever they went.

AUST

All over the world boys were copying the Beatles—their hairdo, the button-down shirts, knitted ties, and Cuban-heeled boots.

In 1964 the Beatles first movie, *A Hard Day's Night,* opened. The reviews were excellent. It was directed by Richard Lester.

They have the kind of magic that the Marx Brothers have.

Movies with pop stars in them have always been poor. This is different. It's original!

A Hard Day's Night was about the Beatles themselves—but making fun of themselves.

It was about how they felt imprisoned by their own *success.* In the movie they were always being *chased* by fans; they dealt with reporters' nonsense questions; and they were put down by people in power.

In August 1964 they made their first big American tour. The Beatles gave thirty-one performances in twenty-four cities. All attendance records were broken.

I still feel as if someday they'll tear me apart.

I wish we could really see some of the places we're visiting.

The press found the boys well behaved but odd and funny.

What about the movement in Detroit to stamp out the Beatles?

We have a campaign to stamp out Detroit.

How do you and John write music?

We do two things to write a song. First we sit down. Then we think about writing a song.

Everything the Beatles touched turned to money.

The Beatles actually slept on these!

After the Beatles stay in one hotel, the owner cut up their pillows into 160 tiny squares. He sold each one for a dollar.

Anyone working here with a Beatle mop-head hairdo has to wear a hairnet.

In England boys who wore their hair like the Beatles had to wear hairnets in many working places.

Everywhere in the world fans bought Beatle posters, books, magazines, fashions, and wigs.

After *A Hard Day's Night,* the Beatles musical style changed. They sang more ballads and the music was not as simple.

Their music was praised by Duke Ellington and Leonard Bernstein.

The Beatles were different from most other singers and pop groups. They were liked by almost everyone: males, females, children, parents, and grandparents.

After their 1966 tour of the United States, all the Beatles were millionaires. They loved their fame, but it brought troubles too.

I'm afraid that some fan might pull Zak right out of his pram and kidnap him!

What are you doing here?

We wanted to see John's wife and son.

Ringo married his Liverpool sweetheart, Maureen Cox. They had two sons at the time, Zak and Jason.

In 1965 the Beatles were awarded the MBE, Members of the Most Honorable Order of the British Empire, by England's Queen Elizabeth.

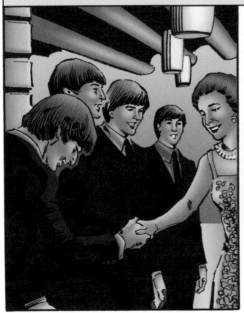

They've brought a lot of money and fame to England.

Just four lucky lads from Liverpool. We export coal but the Queen did not honor the miners with medals.

Many former winners objected to a pop group being so honored. Some sent their medals back.

We love you, Beatles. Yeah! Yeah!

In August 1965 the Beatles appeared at Shea Stadium in New York. The police were keeping busy by picking up fainting girls.

Luckily they don't know this is our last British tour!

We'd have a riot.

In December the Beatles made their last personal appearance tour of England.

Also in August 1965 the Beatles movie *Help!* was released. Richard Lester also directed this movie. It was well received and funny but not as successful as *A Hard Day's Night*.

Help! was a take-off of the British spy stories. It centered on a ring that Ringo was wearing. A mad scientist wanted the ring.

Then John made a public apology. He explained that he had not meant to be disrespectful.

In 1966 *George* Harrison married Patti Boyd, a top British model. Later they went to India.

This is what I want to play, a sitar.

How shall we free ourselves?

Meditate every day.

In India, the Harrisons studied with the Maharishi, a well-known religious teacher. Later all the Beatles worked with him.

They continued to produce hit records and songs: *Revolver, Sgt. Pepper's Lonely Hearts Club Band,* "Strawberry Fields Forever," "Being for the Benefit of Mr. Kite," and "Lucy in the Sky with Diamonds."

The lyrics for "Being for the Benefit of Mr. Kite" were taken from an old English music hall poster.

And the lyrics for "Lucy in the Sky with Diamonds" came from my son, Julian. That's what he called one of his drawings.

People try to find meanings in our songs. Sometimes we don't even know what they mean.

In July, 150 million viewers watched the Beatles TV show, *Our World.*

Look, they are using harpsichords and sitars. They're always full of surprises!

Brian Epstein died suddenly in August 1967. The Beatles missed his friendship and management.

In December 1967 *The Magical Mystery Tour* was shown on British TV. Written, directed, and starring the Beatles, the film showed their inexperience in movie-making. Reviews were poor.

In England they have a "Mystery Tour." You don't know where you're going until you get there. That gave me the idea for this film.

After this TV, show the Beatles announced plans for their new company, Apple Corps. Paul was the head.

We need a business manager.

Aside from recording their own music, they planned to help other people with good ideas.

Apple Corps closed in August 1968. It had been a disappointment.

We were too generous with our money. And the people we trusted were untrained.

In early 1968 all the Beatles went to India to study.

Well, we are not alone. The Maharishi has quite a following: Hollywood movie stars, big shots, and us.

In July 1968 a cartoon movie of the Beatles was released. It was called *The Yellow Submarine.*

This is an easy movie to make. We just watch while the artists draw us.

Well, we do appear for a few minutes. And they use our voices.

This movie showed that music and joy could overcome the enemies of happiness. The Beatles' films were unique.

In 1969 John Lennon was married to Yoko Ono.

Paul McCartney married Linda Eastman, an American photographer.

John has changed. He is interested in strange causes now.

I want to release my solo album *McCartney*.

If you do, it will hurt the sales of *Let It Be*.

More and more, the Beatles were going there separate ways.

I don't like our manager, Allen Klein.

Well, he helped us with our old contract with Epstein.

Let's talk about something nice like our last album *Abbey Road*.

John returned his MBE medal as a protest against the wars in Biafra and Vietnam. He also appeared in an anti-war movie.

In May 1970 the Beatle's movie *Let It Be* was released. None of the Beatles attended the premier. This was a semi-documentary, showing the Beatles working together and fooling around. It also showed John and Paul disagreeing with each other.

In this scene, let's ...

That's a good idea!

They never finish their sentences. Yet they understand each other perfectly!

The Beatles made several albums separately from the group.

My album *McCartney* is doing well.

And so is my single "Give Peace a Chance."

And now I am a composer too. *All Things Must Pass* is doing okay.

I may not have records, but I am in the movies as an actor.

In December 1970 Paul filed a suit in court demanding that the Beatles no longer be considered a group.

I didn't leave the Beatles. The Beatles have left the Beatles, but no one wants to say the party is over.

Any other group could have gotten a replacement for a member who left. But the Beatles were made up of John Lennon, Paul McCartney, George Harrison, and Ringo Starr. No one else would do.

JOHN LENNON

On December 8, 1980, Lennon was shot and killed in New York City. The 1971 song "Imagine" took on a whole new meaning after his death.

RINGO STARR

Starr is active in music, television, and film. Many drummers today list Ringo as an influence.

GEORGE HARRISON

Harrison died of lung cancer on November 21, 2001. He often said, "Everything else can wait but the search for God cannot wait, and love one another."

PAUL MCCARTNEY

Sir Paul is still active in music: classical, electronic, pop, and film scores. He was knighted by Queen Elizabeth II in 1997.

Usage guide for exercise

This book contains a variety of different exercises including translation, fill in the blanks, matching, multiple choices and drawing. Below are the icons and formats that guide readers to complete the exercises.

" ⊕ " means "translation"

You may find it easy to translate the meaning in these exercises. However, it would be wonderful if you could translate them in real Chinese expression. These exercises may help you understand and memorize the English expression more.

" ✐ " means "oral usage"

You will often come across these words or expressions in conversation. Some of them should be avoided in writing.

" _____ * " means "try to compete with your friends"

These are useful phrases or expressions that can be used with different words that you may know. Try to think of as many as possible. To compete with others is a good way to learn more.

" ☼ " Tips help readers to learn more background information and grammar points.

"The thing is, we're all really the same person. We're just four parts of the one." Paul McCartney

1. ✡ The thing is

_____

2. ✡ John Lennon

_____

3. ✡ Paul McCartney

_____

4. ✡ George Harrison

_____

5. ✡ Ringo Starr

_____

The Beatles charted 20 number one singles in the United States—three more than Elvis.

Liverpool is the industrial city in England where the Beatles grew up. **In those days** there were more people **out of** work there than in any other place in the country.

1. "In those days" means

   A. the days when the Beatles were writing their songs
   B. years during which the Beatles were growing up
   C. those days the Beatles were writing about in their songs

2. out of _____ *

Merseyside was a section of Liverpool. It had many clubs where small bands played for teenagers. As many as 350 bands played there **for very little money.**

3. for _____ money *

The *Mersey Beat* was a newspaper known only to local beat music lovers until the Beatles made Liverpool, and the newspaper, famous.

Liverpool had one of the first rock concerts. Alan Williams, the Beatles first manager, held a fourteen hour pop concert outdoors.

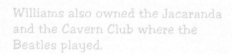

Williams also owned the Jacaranda and the Cavern Club where the Beatles played.

John Lennon

Stay until the baby is born.

1. What is the appropiate answer?

His father is _____.

A. always at home
B. never home
C. sometimes at home
D. usually not at home

John Lennon was born in October 1940. **His father came and went from his life frequently.**

John went to live with his aunt and uncle when he was about 5 years old.

See, Aunt Mimi, I've written a story for you. And I drew a picture too.

When John was eleven, he heard Bill Haley and the Comets on records. Then he discovered the records of **Elvis Presley.**

2. ✦ Elvis Presley

Are you listening to "Rock Around the Clock" again?

No, something I just got. A singer named Elvis Presley. He's American and great!

John liked to draw. He also enjoyed listening to music.

3. Choose the right answer for the use of could?

I'm glad you came to see me. I want to ask a favour, Mum. **Could** you buy me a guitar?

Well, luv, if I can find an inexpensive one.

A guitar's all right, John, but you'll never earn a living from it.

1. ability
2. politeness
3. permission
4. suggestion
5. possibility

When he was sixteen, John formed a musical group called the Quarrymen. In 1958 his mother was killed by a car. An unhappy John was comforted by his friend Paul McCartney.

30

George Harrison

1. "I dunno" is "I _____"

George, what's wrong at school? I'm getting bad reports.

I dunno. Trouble just finds me, I guess.

2. ✪ Trouble just finds me

_____

George Harrison was born in February 1943. He had a happy home but was a troublemaker at school.

In his teens, George was a British "teddy boy," a tough guy.

My folks are great. But I've got to be independent.

folks don't care if I'm alive or dead.

4. folks means

A. songs
B. parents
C. same nationality
D. friends

3. "a tough guy" means

A. someone who has led a hard life
B. someone physically strong
C. someone who is difficult to understand
D. troublemaker

It took you a long time... interested in music.

Yeah, but I am now... to ask mum for a guitar.

George isn't too young for us. I wasn't much older when I joined last year.

He's mighty good on that guitar. So, okay George.

5. ✪ Beatles

_____

George had no interest in music until he was fourteen. Then Paul McCartney helped him learn to play the guitar.

6. "stood for" means

A. represented
B. played
C. supported
D. provided

George joined the Quarrymen in 1958.

John changed the name of the Quarrymen to the Silver Beatles then to the Beatles. The "beat" in Beatles stood for beat music.

The Beatles played at many of the clubs at Merseyside. John, Paul, and George were joined by Stuart Sutcliffe on guitar and Tommy Moore on the drums.

In 1960 Allan Williams, their manager, got them a date to play at a music club in Hamburg, Germany. Tommy was replaced on the drums by Pete Best.

They're making so much noise. They can't hear us.

They don't understand the words in English anyway. Just pound the chords and **scream the lyrics**.

the German soldier! March, march!

Let's all imitate the soldiers by high-stepping.

At their drinking and dancing clubs the Germans wanted loud music with a good beat. The Beatles gave them this.

1. ⊕ **scream the lyrics**

_____

2. "fool around" mean "behave in a _____ way"

   A. serious
   B. selfish
   C. dangerous
   D. playful

The Germans loved to see the Beatles **fool around** and make fun of Hitler.

The Beatles were overtired, often playing for eight hours a day, seven days a week. They lived in run-down apartments behind the club where they performed.

While they were playing for a rival nightclub, it was reported that George Harrison was underage. Without a work permit, George was deported home to England. Except for Stuart, who left the band in Hamburg, the rest of the Beatles soon followed George home.

During this time a record store manager, Brian Epstein, was receiving many requests for a group he had never heard of. He started to make inquiries.

Epstein wanted to see what all they fuss was about. He went to a lunchtime concert at the Cavern Club down the street from his shop. Epstein thought that the band had great potential.

1. "during this time" usually refer to

A. an hour
B. this moment
C. indifinite period of time
D. a day

2. _____ requests *

3. down the _____ *

The Beatles agreed and a contract was signed on January 24, 1962.

I saw your performance, and I think you have something special. I want to be your manager.

I wouldn't touch that band with a barge pole! They didn't pay me my commission.

Epstein set out to change the Beatles' image. He believed a more clean-cut appearance would help the band become more accepted by the general public.

4. matching

set out   •   • a company

set up   •   • a plan

set forth •   • two distinguish

set apart •   • on a journey

That's not the look I want for all of you. I'll pick new clothes for you to wear.

Brian got in touch with Allan Williams, who was no longer the Beatles' manager. He wanted to make sure that Williams did not have any ties to the band.

Epstein tried to interest several recording companies in the Beatles. They **turned** him **down**.

You **should** realize that the Beatles will be bigger than Presley.

Go back to your store business, Brian.

Finally Epstein persuaded George Martin of EMI to listen to the Beatles.

1. turn down a _____ *

They have something! Yes, I'll be their recording manager.

2. Choose the right answer for the use of should?

1. certainty
2. advice
3. order
4. politeness
5. opinion 6. decision

John, Paul, and George began to be a little upset with Pete Best.

We're a group for...

He acts like he's a one-man band.

Martin insisted that Pete Best did not fit into the group. Epstein liked Pete but had to let him go.

I'm sorry, Pete. But we have to do what EMI says.

I'll find work.

In August 1962 Ringo Starr became the Beatles' drummer. He was later called "the luckiest unknown drummer in the world." But as the fourth Beatle, Ringo Starr **held his own with the others.**

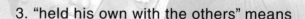

3. "held his own with the others" means

A. better than the others
B. considered to be an equal with the others
C. supported the others
D. opposed the others

1. Ringo's mother has <u>no/one/two/more</u>
   <u>than two kid/kids.</u>

Ringo Starkey was born in July 1940. He became Ringo Starr.

I wish I had a brother or sister to play with.

You're enough for us! But I wish we had a bathroom.

2. ✪ You're enough for us!

Due to several illnesses, Ringo was in and out of the hospital until he was a teenager.

He's still too weak to go home yet.

3. Do you know some more similar structures such as "in and out"?
   _____ and _____*

Ringo met the Beatles in Hamburg. He was playing with another group.

...club too. Those rooms are worse than these. I'll take the conditions in Liverpool any day.

Do you like Liverpool better because of a hairdresser named Maureen Cox?

36

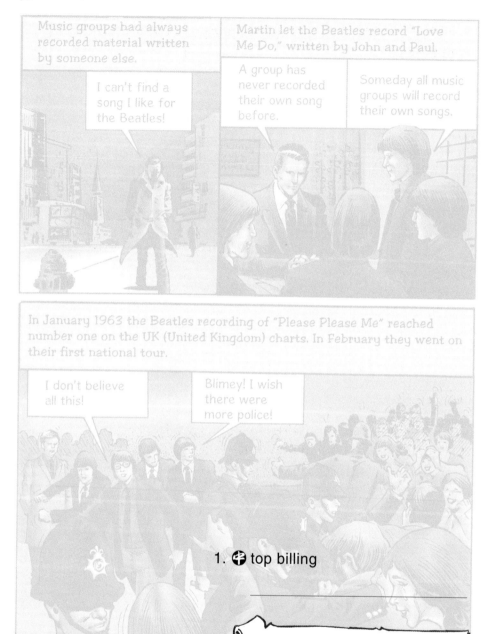

1. 🎯 top billing

In May, on their third tour, they had **top billing**. It was then that Beatlemania—the fans screaming, fainting, and rioting—began.

In October the Beatles appeared on British TV.

They bloody well better let me in. I've been here all day.

The show was called *Sunday Night at the London Palladium*. The theater was mobbed all day.

When they returned from a successful tour of Sweden, the airport was mobbed.

Blimey! I've never seen anything like this in my life!

In November they appeared on The *Royal Variety Show*. Queen Elizabeth, the Queen Mother, Princess Margaret, and Lord Snowden attended.

Those of you in the cheaper seats clap your hands, and those of you in the expensive seats just rattle your jewelry.

There were 250,000 advance orders for the Beatles' second album, *With the Beatles*, beating Elvis Presley's *Blue Hawaii*.

There were one million advance orders for their single "I Want to Hold Your Hand."

In December after the *Beatles Christmas Show*, the *London Times* called the Beatles "the outstanding English composers of 1963."

The *Sunday Times* called them "the greatest composers since Beethoven."

When the Beatles had four solid hits in America, Brian Epstein booked their first United States visit. Ten thousand fans greeted them at Kennedy Airport.

On February 9, 1964, seventy-three million people watched the Beatles on the *Ed Sullivan Show*.

I love their accents!

I just love them!

The Washington Coliseum was jammed for their concert.

They're too noisy to hear us.

When they scream, I just pretend to sing the words.

After the concert, the British Embassy gave a party for them. One girl cut off a piece of Ringo's hair.

After two sell-out shows at Carnegie Hall in New York, the Beatles appeared on a second *Ed Sullivan Show* in Miami Beach.

After it was over, they rested on a private boat.

This is the life!

The police sergeant who was in charge of their security invited them to his house for dinner.

We thought you should see what most of America is like.

1. "This is the life!" means

A. we are so fortunate
B. life is short
C. things could be so much better
D. I want so much more out of life

1. point out

1. mop-head hairdo,
2. button-down shirts,
3. knitted ties,
4. Cuban-heeled boots

on the picture

All over the world boys were copying the Beatles—their **hairdo, the button-down shirts, knitted ties**, and **Cuban-heeled boots**.

In 1964 the Beatles first movie, *A Hard Day's Night*, opened. The reviews were excellent. It was directed by Richard Lester.

They have the kind of magic that the Marx Brothers have.

Movies with pop stars in them have always been poor. This is different. It's original!

A Hard Day's Night was about the Beatles themselves—but making fun of themselves.

1. "put down" means

A. accepted
B. studied
C. criticized
D. invited

It was about how they felt imprisoned by their own success. In the movie they were always being chased by fans; they dealt with reporters' nonsense questions; and they were **put down** by people in power.

In August 1964 they made their first big American tour. The Beatles gave thirty-one performances in twenty-four cities. All attendance records were broken.

1. Choose the right answer for the use of could?

1. ability
2. politeness
3. permission
4. suggestion
5. possibility

I still feel as if tear me apart.

I wish we **could** really see some of the places we're visiting.

The press found the boys well behaved but odd and funny.

What about the movement in Detroit to stamp out the Beatles?

We have a campaign to stamp out Detroit.

How do you and John write music?

We do two things to write a song. First we sit down. Then we think about writing a song.

Everything the Beatles touched turned to money.

The Beatles actually slept on these!

Anyone working here with a Beatle mop-head hairdo has to wear a hairnet.

After the Beatles stay in one hotel, the owner cut up their pillows into 160 tiny squares. He sold each one for a dollar.

In England boys who wore their hair like the Beatles had to wear hairnets in many working places.

Everywhere in the world fans bought Beatle posters, books, magazines, fashions, and wigs.

After *A Hard Day's Night,* the Beatles musical style changed. They sang more ballads and the music was not as simple.

> I still love their first records. *She loves you, yeah, yeah, yeah.*

> But have you heard Paul's song "Yesterday?" It's about lost love.

> Have you heard the album *Rubber Soul?*

Their music was praised by Duke Ellington and Leonard Bernstein.

> The Beatles? Great man. Just great.

> The Beatles? The most original group to **come along in years.** Great!

1. 😊 man

_____

2. **"come along" means**

A. go together
B. get better
C. follow
D. emerge

The Beatles were different from most other singers and pop groups. They were liked by almost everyone: males, females, children, parents, and grandparents.

3. **"in years" means**

A. in a few years
B. in many years
C. in those years
D. in several years

After their 1966 tour of the United States, all the Beatles were millionaires. They loved their fame, but it brought troubles too.

I'm afraid that some fan might pull Zak right out of his pram and kidnap him!

Ringo married his Liverpool sweetheart, Maureen Cox. They had two sons at the time, Zak and Jason.

What are you doing here?

We wanted to see John's wife and son.

In 1965 the Beatles were awarded the MBE, Members of the Most Honorable Order of the British Empire, by England's Queen Elizabeth.

1. ✪ lads

They've brought a lot of money and fame to England.

Just four lucky **lads** from Liverpool. We export coal but the Queen did not honor the miners with medals.

2. "sent his medal back" means
"_____ his medal"

Many former winners objected to a pop group being so honored. Some **sent their medals back**.

We love you, Beatles. Yeah! Yeah!

1. "We'd" is a short form of "we _____"

We'd have a riot.

know this is our last British tour!

A. avoid being idle
B. try hard
C. accomplish a lot
D. feel busy

In August 1965 the Beatles appeared at Shea Stadium in New York. The police were **keeping busy** by picking up fainting girls.

2. "We'd" is a short form of "we _____"

In December the Beatles made their last personal appearance tour of England.

A. should
B. had
C. could
D. would

Also in August 1965 the Beatles movie *Help!* was released. Richard Lester also directed this movie. It was wonderful and funny but not as successful as *A Hard Day's Night*.

3. What can have a take-off besides aeroplanes? _____ *

Help! was a **take-off** of the British spy stories. It centered on a ring that Ringo was wearing. A mad scientist wanted the ring.

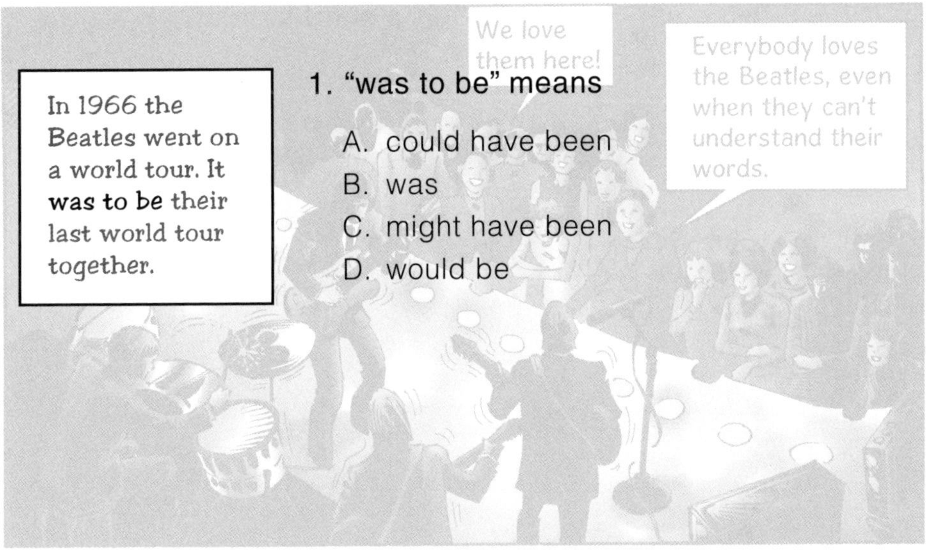

We love them here!

Everybody loves the Beatles, even when they can't understand their words.

In 1966 the Beatles went on a world tour. It **was to be** their last world tour together.

1. "was to be" means

A. could have been
B. was
C. might have been
D. would be

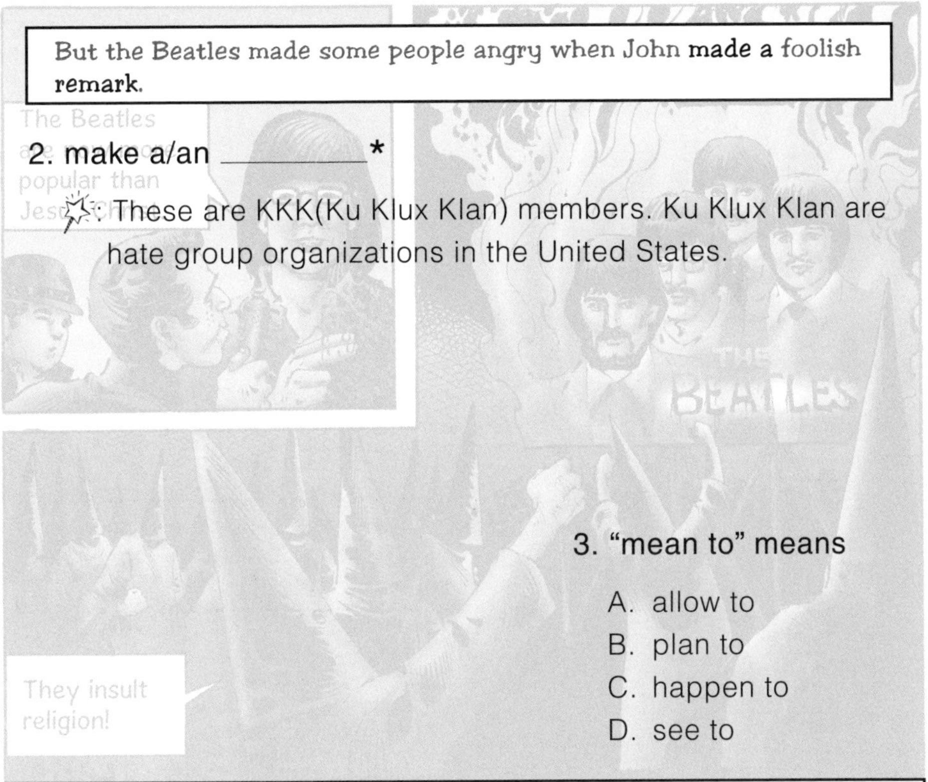

But the Beatles made some people angry when John **made a** foolish **remark**.

The Beatles are more popular than Jesus.

2. make a/an _____ *

☆: These are KKK(Ku Klux Klan) members. Ku Klux Klan are hate group organizations in the United States.

3. "mean to" means

A. allow to
B. plan to
C. happen to
D. see to

They insult religion!

Then John made a public apology. He explained that he had not **meant to** be disrespectful.

In 1966 George Harrison married Patti Boyd, a top British model. Later they went to India.

This is what I want to play, a sitar.

How shall we free ourselves?

Meditate every day.

In India, the Harrisons studied with the Maharishi, a well-known religious teacher. Later all the Beatles worked with him.

They continued to produce hit records and songs: *Revolver, Sgt. Pepper's Lonely Hearts Club Band,* "Strawberry Fields Forever," "Being for the Benefit of Mr. Kite," and "Lucy in the Sky with Diamonds."

The lyrics for "Being for the Benefit of Mr. Kite" were taken from an old English music hall poster.

And the lyrics for "Lucy in the Sky with Diamonds" came from my son, Julian. That's what he called one of his drawings.

People try to find meanings in our songs. Sometimes we don't even know what they mean.

In July, 150 million viewers watched the Beatles TV show, *Our World.*

1. full of _____*

Look, they are using harpsichords and sitars. They're always **full of** surprises!

Brian Epstein died suddenly in August 1967. The Beatles **missed his** friendship and management.

1. **miss his** ———— *
(words with -ship, -ness, -ment etc)

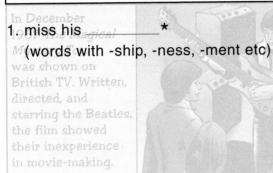

In December 1967, *The Magical Mystery Tour* was shown on British TV. Written, directed, and starring the Beatles, the film showed their inexperience in movie-making. Reviews were poor.

In England they have a "Mystery Tour." You don't know where you're going until you get there. That gave me the idea for this film.

After this TV show, the Beatles announced plans for their new company, Apple Corps. Paul was the head.

We need a business manager.

Aside from recording their own music, they planned to help other people with good ideas.

Apple Corps closed in August 1968. It had been a disappointment.

We were too generous with our money. And the people we trusted were untrained.

2. ✪ **big shots**

In early 1968 all the Beatles went to India to study.

Well, we are not alone. The Maharishi has quite a following: Hollywood movie stars, **big shots**, and us.

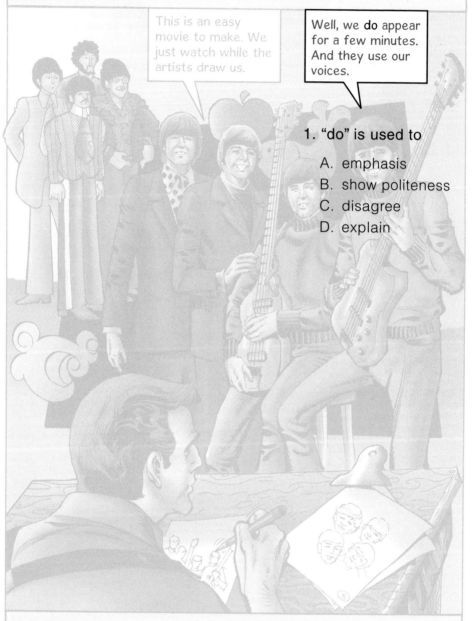

In July 1968 a cartoon movie of the Beatles was released. It was called *The Yellow Submarine.*

This is an easy movie to make. We just watch while the artists draw us.

Well, we **do** appear for a few minutes. And they use our voices.

1. "do" is used to

A. emphasis
B. show politeness
C. disagree
D. explain

This movie showed that music and joy could overcome the enemies of happiness. The Beatles' films were unique.

In 1969 John Lennon was married to Yoko Ono.

Paul McCartney married Linda Eastman, an American photographer.

John has changed. He is interested in strange causes now.

I want to release my solo album *McCartney*.

If you do, it will hurt the sales of *Let It Be*.

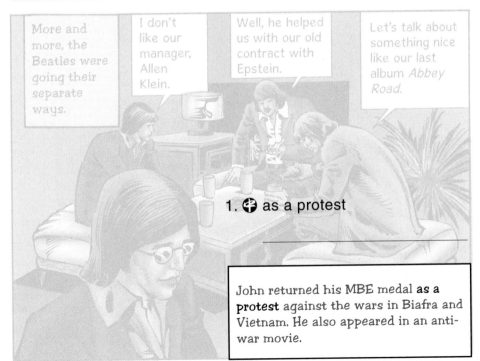

More and more, the Beatles were going their separate ways.

I don't like our manager, Allen Klein.

Well, he helped us with our old contract with Epstein.

Let's talk about something nice like our last album *Abbey Road*.

1. ⊕ as a protest

_____

John returned his MBE medal **as a protest** against the wars in Biafra and Vietnam. He also appeared in an anti-war movie.

In May 1970 the Beatle's movie *Let It Be* was released. None of the Beatles attended the premier. This was a semi-documentary, showing the Beatles working together and fooling around. It also showed John and Paul disagreeing with each other.

In this scene, let's ...

That's a good idea!

They never finish their sentences. Yet they understand each other perfectly!

The Beatles made several albums separately from the group.

My album *McCartney* is doing well.

And so is my single "Give Peace a Chance."

And now I am a composer too. *All Things Must Pass* is doing okay.

I may not have records, but I am in the movies as an actor.

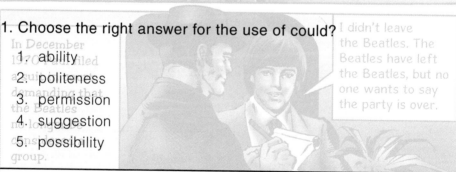

I didn't leave the Beatles. The Beatles have left the Beatles, but no one wants to say the party is over.

In December 1974 Lennon filed a suit... demanding that the Beatles no longer be considered a group.

1. Choose the right answer for the use of could?

1. ability
2. politeness
3. permission
4. suggestion
5. possibility

Any other group **could** have gotten a replacement for a member who left. But the Beatles were made up of John Lennon, Paul McCartney, George Harrison, and Ringo Starr. No one else would do.

JOHN LENNON

On December 8, 1980, Lennon was shot and killed in New York City. The 1971 song "Imagine" took on a whole new meaning after his death.

RINGO STARR

Starr is active in music, television, and film. Many drummers today list Ringo as an influence.

GEORGE HARRISON

Harrison died of lung cancer on November 21, 2001. He often said, "Everything else can wait but the search for God cannot wait, and love one another."

PAUL MCCARTNEY

Sir Paul is still active in music: classical, electronic, pop, and film scores. He was knighted by Queen Elizabeth II in 1997.

Answers

Page 27
1 open answer
2 open answer
3 open answer
4 open answer
5 open answer

Page 28
1 B
2 order, stock, date, job...
3 a lot of, some, less,
   more, ... ; easy,

Page 29
1 C
2 open answer
3 politeness

Page 31
1 I don't know
2 open answer
3 D
4 B
5 A
6 open answer

Page 32
1 open answer
2 D

Page 33
1 C
2 making, answering, ...
3 corner, road, corridor, ...
4 set out
   <--> a plan,
   set up
   <--> a co
   <--> on a journey,
   set apart
    <--> two distinguish

Page 34
1 opinion
2 proposal, suggestion, ...
3 B

Page 35
1 one

2 open answer
3 on and off, back and forth...

Page 36
1 open answer

Page 38
1 A

Page 39
1 open answer

Page 40
1 C

Page 41
1 possibility

Page 42
1 open answer
2 D
3 B

Page 43
1 returned
2 open answer

Page 44
1 A
2 C
3 economy, love life, career...

Page 45
1 D
2 apology, statement, request,
   living, inquiry, anouncement...
----
3 B

Page 46
1 love, fun, distress, rubbish...

Page 47
1 companionship, guidence,
   leadership...
2 open answer

Page 48
1 A

Page 49
1 open answer

Page 50
1 possibility

General vocabulary

Page No.	Vocabulary	Parts of Speech	Meaning
6	imitate	verb	模仿
7	contract	noun	合約
7	fuss	verb/noun	大驚小怪
7	potential	noun	潛質
7	commission	noun	佣金
7	I wouldn't touch it with a bargepole		(英國) 我才不會去碰它
7	image	noun	形像
7	appearance	noun	外表
11	rattle	verb	弄出格格響聲
11	mob	verb	團團圍着
11	advanced order	noun	預訂
12	accent(s)	noun	口音
12	coliseum	noun	體育館
12	security	noun	保安
14	review(s)	noun	評論
15	attendance record(s)	noun	上座紀錄
15	wig	noun	假髮
17	kidnap	verb	綁架
17	millionaire	noun	百萬富翁
17	fame	noun	名譽
17	medal	noun	勳章
18	riot	noun	暴動
20	meditate	verb	冥想
20	viewer	noun	觀眾
22	unique	adj	獨特
23	sale(s)	noun	銷售
24	semi-documentary	noun	半紀錄片
25	knight	noun	封爵

Music and performance related vocabulary

Page No.	Vocabulary	Parts of Speech	Meaning
1	single(s)	noun	單曲
1	number one single	noun	冠軍歌曲
2	band	noun	樂隊
2	rock	noun	搖滾
2	pop concert	noun	流行樂會
3	record	noun	唱片
4	banjo	noun	班卓琴
5	beat	noun	節拍
6	lyrics	noun	歌詞
7	performance	noun	表演
10	chart	noun	排行榜
10	fan	noun	歌迷
10	Beatlemania	noun	Beatles迷
	mania	noun	狂躁症
12	composer	noun	作曲家
12	hit(s)	noun	暢銷熱門歌曲
12	sell-out show	noun	滿座表演
16	ballad(s)	noun	情歌/敘事詩
16	album(s)	noun	唱片專輯
20	sitar	noun	西塔琴
20	harpsichord	noun	大鍵琴
23	solo	noun	獨唱
24	premier(premiere)	noun	首演
	attend premiere	noun	出席首演

Activities

The Beatles Hits

The Beatles charted many number one singles in the United States – three more than Elvis. Ask your parents or relatives if they know how to sing the songs below.

U.S. Billboard Chart

Debut Date	Title	Position
January 18, 1964	I Want To Hold Your Hand	1
January 25, 1964	She Loves You	1
March 28, 1964	Can't Buy Me Love	1
July 18, 1964	A Hard Day's Night	1
December 5, 1964	I Feel Fine	1
February 20, 1965	Eight Days A Week	1
April 24, 1965	Ticket To Ride	1
July 31, 1965	Help!	1
September 18, 1965	Yesterday	1
December 11, 1965	We Can Work It Out	1
June 11, 1966	Paperback Writer	1
February 18, 1967	Penny Lane	1
July 22, 1967	All You Need Is Love	1
December 2, 1967	Hello Goodbye	1
September 14, 1968	Hey Jude	1
May 10, 1969	Get Back	1
October 18, 1969	Something	1
March 21, 1970	Let It Be	1
May 23, 1970	The Long And Winding Road	1

See how the Beatles talks about the Beatles

"We were all on this ship in the sixties, our generation, a ship going to discover the New World. And the Beatles were in the crow's nest of that ship."

— John Lennon

"You have to be a bastard to make it, and that's a fact. And the Beatles are the biggest bastards on earth. "

— John Lennon

"I can't deal with the press; I hate all those Beatles questions. "

— Paul McCartney

"Somebody said to me, 'But the Beatles were anti-materialistic.' That's a huge myth. John and I literally used to sit down and say, 'Now, let's write a swimming pool.' "

— Paul McCartney

"As far as I'm concerned, there won't be a Beatles reunion as long as John Lennon remains dead."

— George Harrison

"The Beatles saved the world from boredom. "

— George Harrison

"We will miss George for his sense of love, his sense of music and his sense of laughter. "

— Ringo Starr

Recommended Readers

Fiction: Black Cat

Level 1
Peter Pan
Zorro!
American Folk Tales
The True Story of Pocahontas
Davy Crockett
Great Expectations
Rip Van Winkle and The Legend of Sleepy Hollow
The Happy Prince and The Selfish Giant
The American West
Halloween Horror
The Adventures of Tom Sawyer
The Adventures of Huckleberry Finn
The Wonderful Wizard of Oz
The Secret of the Stones
The Wind in the Willows
The Black Arrow
Around the World in Eighty Days
Little Women
Beauty and the Beast
Black Beauty

Level 2
Oliver Twist
King Authur and his Knights
Oscar Wilde's Short Stories
Robin Hood
British and American Festivities
David Copperfield
Animal Tales
The Fisherman and his Soul
The Call of the Wild
Ghastly Ghosts!

Level 3
Alice's Adventures in Wonderland
The Jumping Frog
Hamlet
The Secret Garden
Great English Monarchs and their Times
True Adventure Stories

Level 4
The £1,000,000 Bank Note
Jane Eyre
Sherlock Holmes Investigates
Gulliver's Travels
The Strange Case of Dr Jekyll and Mr Hyde
Romeo and Juliet
Treasure Island
The Phantom of the Opera
Classic Detective Stories
Alien at School

Level 5
A Christmas Carol
The Tragedy of Dr Faustus
Washington Square
A Midsummer Night's Dream
American Horror
Much Ado about Nothing
The Canterbury Tales
Dracula
The Last of the Mohican
The Big Mistake and Other Stories
The Age of Innocence

Level 6
Pride and Prejudice
Robinson Crusoe
A Tale of Two Cities
Frankenstein
The X-File: Squeeze
Emma
The Scarlet Letter
Tess of the d'Urbervilles
The Murders in the Rue Morgue and the Purloined Letter
The Problem of Cell 13

Non-Fiction:
National Geographic

Level 1
The Greatest Creatures on Earth
Amazing Homes we Choose to Live in

Level 2
Living Legends
True Adventures and Exciting Sports

Level 3
Who are the real winners?
Discovering Special Cultures

Level 4
Changing Climates and Natural Habitats
Creativity in Environmental Protection